Summit Elementary Library
1450 W. Countryside Lane
Bloomington, IN 47403

Quiet!
There's a Canary in the Library

Story and Pictures by

DON FREEMAN

QUIET! THERE'S A CANARY IN THE LIBRARY

GOLDEN GATE JUNIOR BOOKS
San Carlos · California

To
Julia Cunningham

Library of Congress catalog card number 69-15398

10 11 12 13 14 15 16 17 18 R 95 94 93 92 91 90 89 88

Every Saturday morning a girl named Cary went to the library.

Before selecting a book, Cary always had a chat with Mrs. Curtis, the librarian.

One Saturday morning she sat down at a small round table between two boys and began looking at a book about the zoo.

After a while Cary slowly closed her book and started talking silently to herself.

“If I were a librarian I know what I would do,” she said.

"I would have a special day when only animals and birds would be allowed to come in and browse."

First, I'll hang this banner outside.

Then I'll sit here behind my desk and wait.

Welcome to my library, Canary. How very nice of you to come so early.

And oh, Lion, I'm so glad you dropped by.

I'm sure you know the rules. No roaring indoors.

Do come in, Bear. There are many books about bears
I know you'll enjoy pawing through.

Here are a few.

I'm so sorry about the door, Elephant. Please let me help you.

You'll need more than four chairs and a table of your own.
I want you to be perfectly comfortable.

I'm very proud to see you, Peacock. I was hoping you'd come today.

To tell the truth, Turtle, I didn't hear you come in.
What a lovely surprise. Do make yourself at home.

Oh my! A giraffe!
I hadn't planned on you popping in so soon.

You'll find some tall tales up there on the top shelf. Do help yourself.

A porcupine! How divine.

Just see that you don't get too close to Lion. They say he's very ticklish.

Gracious me! I didn't expect a whole family of monkeys.
Now promise you'll try to behave. This is a library, not a zoo, you know.

If I let a horse come in

I suppose I'll have to allow a cow to come in, too.

Now, isn't this wonderful? Everyone loves my library.

They're all being as quiet as mice . . .

MICE!

Oh horrors! I should have closed the door!

They're racing up the elephant's trunk.

And now they've frightened my canary.

Oh dear! I told that porcupine not to get too near the lion.

Please, Bear! You must treat those books with care.

I've never heard such a rumpus!

Lion is roaring, Bear is growling, Cow is mooing and Peacock is screeching.

Oh, Canary! What will we do now? And how can I ever get them to leave?

Oh, thank you, Canary.

Listen, everyone! The canary is SINGING.

I do believe she's telling them it's time to go!

Good-by, everyone. I do hope you've enjoyed yourselves.

But remember, as you leave – PLEASE TRY TO BE VERY . . .

"Who, me?" said one of the boys at the table. "I wasn't making any noise."

When Cary realized she had spoken out loud, she was terribly embarrassed.

After a few minutes, she went over to the bookshelf and chose another book to take home

“I hope you will enjoy this bird story,” said Mrs. Curtis cheerfully.

"Oh, I know I shall," whispered Cary.

"Canaries are among my very truest friends."

And out the door she flew.